Oh Megan

I stood in the hallway of my high school chatting up hot Megan with the amazing ass and perky b cup titties. It was after school when I asked her if she would like to come over for dinner sometime.

Megan said sure I'd love to come over to your house for dinner sometime. I said cool, I will let you know when. She flashed me her beautiful smile on her pretty face.

I couldn't believe it, Megan agreed to come to dinner at my house. I thought I'd better tell my white mommy Megan about this as soon as possible.

The next day, I woke up early
and took a shower. I thought
of big booty Megan coming
over for dinner sometime
soon. I became aroused
thinking of her sexy ass. I
stepped out of the shower and
turned. There was my white
mommy Megan standing there
looking at my hard-black
cock.

Megan said oh my god your
naked and your hard as shit.
I said I know you've seen a
cock before that's when she
said I've seen a cock before
but never one as big as yours
or a black one. I said wow,
I'm happy to be the first
black cock that you have
seen.

I said it's not going to go
down with you staring at my

cock, Megan. She said oh god
I'm sorry for staring but you
have quite the penis there.
I said thank you and she said
I'll go make us breakfast.

Megan left and I watched her
sexy big booty jiggle away
from me towards the door then
disappeared down the hallway.
I got ready for school.

I went downstairs to eat
breakfast and it smelt good
as shit. We sat down to eat
breakfast like normal. Megan
was smiling at me and
unusually happy.

Megan said I'm sorry about
drooling on your big black
cock earlier, it's just that
I haven't seen a cock in a

while, so I was a little star
struck by it.

I said I don't mind you
looking at my cock, you are a
beautiful white girl. Megan
said thanks I'm glad you
don't mind me looking at it,
baby.

I said my pleasure, Megan.
We finished up our breakfast
and I was about to take off.
Megan hugged me tight, kissed
me on the cheek then said
have a good day at school
sweetie.

When I came home Megan was
wearing a very sexy outfit.
It was a short white skirt
and a sexy cleavage red t-
shirt that showed off her big

melons for my viewing
pleasure.

I hugged her tight and felt
her melons along with her
hard nipples on my chest. I
said you look so hot Megan,
she said thanks baby I'm glad
you like it.

Later, after we ate dinner,
Megan disappeared then
reappeared in a sexy see-
through robe that was very
revealing. I could see her
big tits and red panties
through the white robe.

I thought damn, I want to hit
that really bad, and I want
to fuck Megan at school too.
I said I want to ask you
something Megan. She said
sure anything.

I said can I have a friend
from school over for dinner
this weekend maybe Saturday.
Megan said sure honey, I can
make us all dinner. I said
that is great, thank you. I
hugged her tight and she held
me close with a loving
embrace.

I said her name is Megan too.
My white mommy smiled and
said cool, I like her name
giggling. I replied, me too,
smiling at her pretty face.

Megan said we should go to
bed. I said I agree. I
followed Megan's sexy
jiggling ass up the stairs
mesmerized by her amazing
cheeks.

She went to her room, and I
went to mine. I went to
sleep quickly because I
couldn't wait for the next
day to tell Megan at school.

I felt my chest being
massaged and I heard my white
mommy say wake up honey
you're going to be late for
school. I woke up
immediately and said oh crap
what time is it, Megan told
me the time and it was still
early. I said oh crap I
forgot to set the alarm.

Megan said good thing I set
my alarm 10 minutes before
yours so when I didn't hear
it this morning. I knew you
weren't awake.

I threw the covers off and I
was hard of course. Megan
saw my boner again and she
said damn that big cock is
always hard.

I said yeah, I need to take a
shower. Megan said I'll go
make us breakfast for my
horny senior and I laughed.
I took a quick shower and
went down to Megan.

I hugged her from behind
lovingly and said thanks for
breakfast. She said you're
welcome sweetie. We sat down
to eat smiling at each other.
I said I can't wait to tell
Megan that you will make us
dinner this Saturday.

Megan hugged me tight and
gave me a quick peck on the

lips before I left for
school. I went to Megan's
locker and told her that she
could come over for dinner
this Saturday.

She said that's great and
hugged me tight. It was our
first hug after flirting all
year. I was happy that she
was still coming. I texted
my white mommy that Megan was
going to be over at 8 pm on
Saturday.

Dinner night, I put on a
white dress shirt and a pair
dress slacks. I waited
nervously; Megan wore a
little black dress that said
fuck me please. The doorbell
finally rang, I walked
nervously to the door.

I opened the door with my
white mommy behind me. I
said wow Megan you look
amazing. My fellow senior
Megan was wearing the same
fuck me dress as my white
mommy but with a lot less
cleavage.

Megan hugged me tight and
said thanks for inviting me
to dinner. When we broke the
hug, I said this is my white
mommy, Megan. They hugged
tight and then Megan said I
didn't know you had a white
mommy. I said now you know
smiling at both of them

My white mommy said dinner is
ready, we all went to the
dining room to be seated and
eat. Megan told my white
mommy that she loved her

dress and my white mommy said
I like your dress too.

My white mommy served us all
dinner. It smelt amazing and
tasted amazing too. Megan is
a wonderful cook.

We all ate in silence while
smiling at each other the
whole time. Megan told my
white mommy that the food was
delicious, and my white mommy
said thank you sweetheart.

My white mommy said why don't
you show Megan your room
honey while I do the dishes
and clean up around here. I
said thank you and I took
Megan up to my bedroom.

I opened the door and Megan
walked in. She saw the big
poster of her on my wall then
she laughed. I have a poster
of you on my wall in my
bedroom at home too.

I said wow what a
coincidence. Megan said I've
had a crush on you since the
9th grade. I said wow I've
had a crush on you since the
9th grade too. Megan said do
you want to make out.

I said hell yeah baby. We
sat on the bed and held hands
looking at each other in the
eyes passionately. We both
leaned in, and the fireworks
started. It felt fucking
intense making out with Megan
for the first time.

We held each other tight, and
our tongues did the dance of
love. Megan pulled me over
on her hot body. I kissed
her neck as I grind my hard
cock into her pussy.

Megan whispered that I'm very
wet and I don't have any
panties on. I moaned wow
Megan, I reached down to rub
her pussy and massaged it
good. I pushed my middle
finger into Megan's wet
pussy, and she moaned with
pleasure as I fingered her
moist pussy.

Megan said I really like you
and I like you fingering my
pussy, but I want some
penetration from your big
black cock. I said are you
sure baby. Megan said yeah,
I've been wanting you to fuck

me since the 9th grade, please
fuck me now.

I spread Megan's sweet white
thighs wide and put my hard
cock at the entrance to a
pussy I've desired for years.
Megan stroked my cock and
rubbed my cockhead between
her pussy lips. The feeling
was intoxicating.

She put it at the entrance to
her pussy and I pushed it
hard penetrating her pussy
deep. Megan moaned as I
entered her. I looked up and
saw my white mommy watching
from the doorway.

I started massaging Megan's
tight white vagina with my
erect penis. It felt better
than any fantasy that I had

of her. The fact that my
white mommy was watching me
have sex with Megan for the
first time really turned me
on and added extra juice to
the situation.

Megan moaned oh god you're so
big baby and so deep, I love
your big fucking cock. A few
more strokes and Megan
creamed my dick as I fucked
her slowly. After she came,
I fucked her harder trying to
come in her pussy.

Megan said oh yeah baby fill
me with your hot sperm, I
want it bad. I held her hips
and fucked her harder. I
could feel my orgasm start
and I let myself go inside of
Megan. I ejaculated inside
of Megan and my orgasm
electrified my entire body.

I leaned down to kiss Megan,
and she held me tight. We
kissed, talked, and held each
other for a while not wanting
to let go. But then Megan
said I need to go home before
my mother comes looking for
her daughter. I said yeah,
we straightened up then went
downstairs. My white mommy
was on the couch waiting for
us. She asked Megan if she
was my girlfriend now.

Megan said I hope so with a
picture of me on his wall and
his warm sperm in my vagina.
I said she is my girlfriend
with my picture on her wall
and her cream on my penis.

My white mommy said I hope
you're on birth control.
Megan said I am on birth
control, not ready for kids
yet there is still college

and a job to go. Megan said
that's great to hear Megan.

Megan said I love your big
breasts, they are amazing,
how big are they. Megan said
38 DD and Megan said wow.
Then she asked if she could
touch them. Megan said sure
go for it, Megan grabbed my
white mommy's big titties and
squeezed them.

Megan said oh wow those are
real and amazingly soft.
Megan said thanks, Megan took
my white mommy's hands and
put them on her small tits.
Megan squeezed her small
titties and she said those
are real too. Megan said I
don't think they make breast
implants this small. We all
laughed out loud.

Megan said I better get home
before my mom sends out the
cavalry. My white mommy said
it was nice meeting you, you
can come over and visit your
boyfriend anytime. Megan
said I'll take you up on that
offer. Megan hugged Megan
then said thanks for a great
evening of food, big tits,
and cock. They smiled at
each other, then Megan hugged
and kissed me goodbye.

I was hard as a rock and felt
up Megan's big ass. I said
I'll see you at school on
Monday. Megan said it will
be our first official day as
boyfriend and girlfriend at
school, I replied I can't
wait, good night sexy.

Megan left and Megan said I
like your new girlfriend. I

said I like her too. Megan
hugged me tight, she said wow
you just fucked your
girlfriend, and your big cock
is hard again.

I said I loved you watching
me fuck Megan. Megan said I
loved watching you fuck her
little white pussy with your
big black cock.

I felt Megan's glorious
cheeks for the first time.
Megan leaned in and kissed me
passionately as I responded
in kind. When we eventually
came up for air. Megan said
we better get to bed. We
have church tomorrow.

I said yes sweet cheeks, I
said you first. I followed
her up the stairs and she

said are you looking at my
big ass. I said I'm looking
at the best ass in
California.

Megan laughed out loud and
said I love you very much. I
said I love you more Megan.
She said good night and I
said good night too sweet
cheeks. Megan smiled at me
lovingly.

I went to bed and drifted off
to sleep as if on cloud nine.
Eight hours later, I woke up
to Megan at my bedside
smiling and wearing a
completely translucent robe.
I could see her delicious
large breast and intoxicating
shaved white vagina.

Megan then sat beside me and
took my hand massaging it
lovingly before putting it in
her mouth to suck my middle
finger, it felt very erotic
in her hot mouth as she
sucked it slowly.

Megan took it out and said
finger me sweetie. She
spread her sweet white thighs
so I could see her pretty
white pussy for the first
time. I wasted no time
inserting my black middle
finger into her little white
vagina.

I started massaging her wet
pussy in and out. Megan
began to moan in the most
pleasurable of manner. I
enjoyed fingering her little
white pussy making her feel
really good. Megan loved it

more and more the longer I
did it. She became
overwhelmed through her head
back and creamed my finger as
an orgasm ravished her entire
body with pleasure.

Megan took my finger out of
her pussy and sucked it
clean. The pleasure of
watching her do that amazed
me. My black cock was rock
hard as Megan took the covers
off. She wrapped her white
hands around my hard-black
cock and started to stroke my
bone. I moaned as the
pleasure of it hit me all
over.

Megan stroked my erect black
penis with a lot of love and
affection. I thoroughly
enjoyed the hell out of it
until I felt a great deal of

pleasure. My eyes rolled
back into my head as my
orgasm washed over my entire
body. I threw my head back
and I felt an extra warm
sensation on my penis from
Megan's warm mouth as my
ejaculation began.

Megan swallowed it all and
cleaned my penis off. I
couldn't believe it, I said
thanks Megan that was
awesome. She said no thank
you for fingering me and
letting me suck your nice big
black penis. I said thanks
for letting me finger your
white vagina.

Megan said now that's done,
time to get ready for church.
We hurried up and got ready
for church, we hopped into
Megan's Mercedes, and went to

church. When we entered the
church, I saw Megan and her
mom sitting with two open
seats next to them.

Megan said let's sit next to
your girlfriend and her mom.
I sat next to Megan and my
white mommy sat next to me.
I held Megan's hand beside
us. Her mom said I'm Mary
her mom, you must be the
boyfriend who is on her wall.

I said yes that is me, nice
to meet you, Mary. Soon it
was communion time, Megan and
Mary went up first. Megan
whispered in my ears that her
mom knows we had sex last
night. We were on the couch
talking when she spread my
thighs and saw your sperm
oozing out of my vagina.

I said oh boy, Megan said she
said good thing I put you on
birth control or you would
get pregnant. I said I'm
sorry Megan and she said
don't be, I wanted to have
sexual intercourse with you
baby. I've been in love with
you since the 9th grade and I
said I've loved you since the
9th grade too.

Mary and Megan came back.
Megan and I went up for our
communion then came back.

Finally, the church service
was over, we went downstairs
to get something to eat.
Mary cornered me and hugged
me tight. She asked me if I
ejaculated inside of her
daughter last night. I said
yes, I did ejaculate inside
of your daughter Megan's

vagina last night and your
daughter orgasmed on my penis
a few times correspondingly.

Mary said oh my god, your
penis is erect in church,
behave yourself. I held her
tighter, and I said I know
you like that big thing on
you. She moaned oh god I
like it, but I shouldn't like
it. I said its ok Mary,
girls are allowed to like a
hard penis. We held each
other for a while. Mary said
I need to go to confession; I
will see you later.

Megan came to me after her
mother left to go to
confession. She asked where
her mother went, and I told
her she asked if I was the
one that ejaculated my sperm
into her daughter's vagina.

I told her yes it was me who
fill you with my sperm.
Megan giggled then ask did
you get hard when she hugged
you and asked you the
question. I said your mom
felt my full erection and
told me to behave we are in
church.

I told her I know you like
it. Megan said what did she
say to you, she said she
really like it then ran off
to confession. Megan said
that's my mom horny and
uptight laughing.

Megan hugged me and kissed
me. She said oh yeah that's
my horny man, always hard and
ready for vagina. I said you
know it baby.

After church, I went home and hung out with my white mommy until bedtime. I woke up Monday morning as I smelt breakfast. I got ready quickly and ran down to the kitchen.

Megan was wearing a French maid apron and that was it. I dropped my pants and hugged her from behind. Megan moaned with pleasure as I massaged her large melons and kissed her neck.

Megan said good morning sweetie, I'm happy that you like my outfit. I put my hand between her sweet white thighs and inserted my middle finger into her wet vagina. I massaged her vagina until I felt her body vibrate with an orgasm.

I kept humping her juicy ass
and Megan said tell me when
you're going to cum, I want
to swallow all of your tasty
warm sperm. Moments later, I
said oh Megan I'm going to
come. She quickly went to
her knees and inhaled my cock
quickly.

I happily ejaculated all of
my warm sperm in her fucking
mouth. Megan swallowed it
like a hungry puppy. I was
very happy and proud of her
for doing that for me. My
white mommy doesn't like a
mess and she made sure there
wasn't one on the floor by
sucking me dry.

I pulled up my pants then we
sat down to eat breakfast.
Megan was smiling and looking
at me as we ate our

breakfast. We hugged and
kissed before I went to
school.

I met Megan at her locker.
She said good morning stud,
she hugged and kissed me in
front of everyone. I was
very surprised that she did
it, wanting everyone to know
that we are now a couple.

I was flushed with lust, good
thing I'm dark or everyone
would notice. I went to my
classes and soon it was lunch
time. Megan waved me over to
sit with her and the rest of
the softball team.

They introduced themselves to
me. I said hello to
everyone, I know I won't
remember all of their names.

Megan rubbed my dick and said
there is a lot of white pussy
at this table, I wonder if
any of them had some big
black dick like I have.

I became hard as she
whispered into my ears.
Megan said I love making you
hard baby. I whispered back
I love being hard for you
babe.

We ate our food smiling and
whispering to each other.
The other girls talked
amongst themselves. When
lunch was over, we finished
the rest of our classes for
the day.

I was at my locker when Megan
came up behind me and
whispered hey stud, you want

some white pussy baby. I
said oh yeah, I always want
you hot stuff. She said this
weekend, I'm coming over for
some penetration by your huge
cock.

We hugged and kissed goodbye
as I had a handful of her
juicy big ass. She left and
I went home. Megan was on
the couch sleeping naked and
her mouth was open.

I dropped my pants and pushed
my black dick into her mouth
as I inserted my middle
finger into her white pussy.
It was the first time that
I've seen her totally naked,
and she has an incredible
body.

Megan started sucking my dick
and moaning as she opened her
pretty blue eyes, fixing her
blonde hair. She spread her
sweet white thighs so that I
may finger her white pussy
better and I did just that to
her.

Megan sucked the hell out of
my dick, and I fucking loved
it. She creamed my finger
like crazy as I finger fucked
her pussy really good. It
wasn't long before I had that
wonderful feeling and filled
her mouth with hot sperm.
She happily swallowed it all
down and kissed my dick. She
said welcome home honey.

I said it's always a pleasure
to come home to you, Megan.
I said Megan is coming over
this weekend for penetration,

I look forward to you
watching us fuck. Megan said
I look forward to watching
you penetrate your
girlfriend's tight white
pussy with your big black
cock until you both have an
orgasm.

Megan and I kissed lovingly.
I went to do my homework.
The weekend took forever to
get there but when it came, I
was happy as a clam with a
pearl.

Megan came over in a short
white skirt and a tight white
t-shirt. She hugged and
kissed me then hugged and
kissed my white mommy. We
sat down and ate dinner then
I took Megan to my bedroom.

I sat on the bed as she took
off her skirt and top. I
took my pants and shirt off
quickly. Megan stood before
me then went to her knees
parting my knees. She
started stroking my cock and
licking my balls. It felt
incredible.

Megan stopped pushed me back
and slid her white pussy down
my black pole. My white
mommy was watching us totally
naked. My flagpole became
fully rigid as Megan fucked
me. I squeezed her little
tits and she fucked me
harder.

Megan moaned oh god I'm
creaming your big fucking
dick. I said oh yeah, my
sexy girlfriend. She said
your turn to get on top.

Megan laid back and I
penetrated her deep again. I
slowly fucked her as we
smiled at each other enjoying
the moment.

Megan saw my white mommy
watching us fuck and told me
so. She told my white mommy
to come sit on the bed and
watch us fuck. Megan came in
and said hi honey to me
smiling.

It really turned me on seeing
my white mommy totally naked
on the bed watching me fuck
my hot girlfriend. I fucked
her harder and harder. Megan
moaned oh god Megan I'm
creaming your black son's
huge cock.

Megan looked at the cream on
my cock and bit her sexy
blowjob lips. I told Megan I
love you watching me fuck my
girlfriend. Megan said I
love watching my black son
pound his white girlfriend
with his big dick.

Megan asked if I ever fucked
my white mommy. I said no
that's when she said I want
to watch you fuck her. I
said really are you sure.
Megan said please, I want to
watch you fuck her until you
ejaculate inside her white
pussy.

I said ok taking my hard cock
out of my girlfriend, Megan.
My white mommy laid down and
I slid between her sweet
white thighs. I held my cock
and slammed it up her cunt.

Megan moaned oh god your big
black cock is inside of me,
fuck me.

I started fucking my white
mommy and she loved it. My
girlfriend said oh my god
this is so hot I'm getting
wetter. She grabbed my white
mommy's big titties and
squeezed them as I fucked her
harder.

It made my white mommy cream
my black cock for the first
time and it was a lot of
cream wow. I said look Megan
she is creaming my dick; I
think she likes it. My white
mommy said I love it more
than you know. My girlfriend
said fuck her harder, cream
pie her, I said oh yeah.

I held Megan's hips and
fucked the shit out of her
tight pussy. Five minutes
later there was a tingle in
my balls, and I said oh god
I'm cumming. My girlfriend
said oh fuck yeah this is
fucking hot as shit, I can't
believe you cream pied your
white mommy.

My white mommy said I love
it; my black's son's huge
cock is deep in my white
vagina ejaculating sperm. I
lean down and kissed my white
mommy after I came in her
tight little pussy.

My girlfriend kissed me
passionately for a little
while then she kissed my
white mommy passionately too.

All three of us laid back in
the bed with me in the
middle. Megan said time to
call my mom and see if she
will come over. I said why
and Megan said so you can
fuck her while I hide under
the bed. My white mommy
laughed out loud then said
that is so kinky, I love your
girlfriend, she is very
naughty.

I said I love the idea, but I
don't think your mom will
come over this late. Megan
said dad is out of town for a
while and I know she must be
horny.

I said call and see what
happens. Megan called her
mom and she answered. Megan
said mom, I know your all
alone at home and I don't

want you to be since I'll be
at my boyfriend's house all
weekend. I'm sure his white
mommy won't mind if you stay
in the guess bedroom.

Mary said ok, if she doesn't
mind, I'll come right over, I
hate being home alone. Megan
hung up and I said oh my god
wow, she is coming over.

Megan whispered into the ears
of my white mommy, but I
couldn't hear what she said
to her. We all put on robes
and waited for Mary.

She came over in a robe too.
I said it's great to see you
again Mary and I hugged her
tight. Megan said I'm glad
you came mom. My white mommy
said I'm glad you came too.

Mary said thank you guys for
the warm welcome.

We sat around and watched a
movie then Mary said I'm
getting sleepy. My white
mommy showed her to the guest
bedroom.

A couple of hours later,
Megan and I snuck into Mary's
room. I dropped my robe and
Megan got on her knees. She
stroked and sucked my dick
until I was fully aroused.

I slithered into the bed of
Mary quietly as Megan
slithered under the bed. I
spooned Mary, I grinded my
hard cock on her big ass and
felt up her small titties.

I kissed her neck and said
wake up Mary. She woke up
and said oh my god what are
you doing in here, you're my
daughter's boyfriend. I said
its ok baby, she is sound
asleep in our bed.

Mary said oh my god your
naked and your big black cock
is on my big ass. I said
don't you like it, I held her
tight and grind my hard cock
into her ass. Mary said oh
god I like it and I'm already
wet. I rubbed her pussy and
stuck my middle finger into
her pussy. Mary said oh god
this feels so good baby.

Mary said I can't believe we
are doing this but get on top
and stick your big black
penis in my white vagina. I
said that's the spirit baby.

Mary laid back and I climbed
on top of her. I held her
tight and kissed her
passionately. She happily
reciprocated my passionate
kissing.

I held her hips and slammed
my hard-black cock up her
married cunt. Mary moaned oh
wow that's the biggest penis
that I have ever felt inside
of me.

I smiled at her and said my
pleasure being your biggest
one. Mary smiled and took
all of me. She said wow this
feels amazing baby don't
stop.

Moments later, Mary
lubricated my cock with her
first orgasm. I said wow you

came, and she said oh yeah,
your big penis is wonderful.
I said your vagina is awesome
too. She giggled and said
you can give it to me harder.
I won't break, I fucked Mary
harder, and she moaned
louder. She creamed my cock
again and she said wow never
came twice with a man before.
It motivated me to fuck her
even harder. Mary massaged
my chest and said my
daughter's boyfriend is such
stud. I moaned and filled
Mary with all of my love.

I said oh wow that was
amazing, I leaned down and
kissed her passionately.
Mary said that was amazing
baby thanks for being my
first black penis.

Megan came out from under the
bed and said so mom, you like
black penis too. Mary
jumped, screamed, and said oh
my god Mary don't tell your
dad that I cheated on him by
having sexual intercourse
with your black boyfriend.

Megan said its ok mom, your
secret is safe with me, I
don't mind you getting along
too well with my boyfriend.
Mary laughed out loud.

Megan came into the room and
said oh wow to Megan, she
said is my black son's penis
in your mother. Megan said
oh yeah and he ejaculated his
hot sperm inside of her too.

Megan said oh wow honey you
ejaculated inside of two

white vagina's tonight. Mary
looked at Megan and Megan
said no not me then pointed
towards my white mommy.
Mary's eyes doubled in size,
and her mouth dropped open.
Megan, Megan, and I nearly
died of laughter.

The end

www.ingramcontent.com/pod-product-compliance
Lightning Source LLC
Chambersburg PA
CBHW072130150726
47999CB00005B/2225